Numb...

Contents

	Page
Counting races	2-3
Counting On	4-5
Guess the Number	6-7
Memory Test	8-9
Number Patterns	10-11
Number Gap	12
Near Doubles	13
Hot Potato	14-15
Age Sums	16

written by Pam Holden

Counting races are always fun. Try to count faster than your friend by using **Shortcut Counting**. Remember that counting doesn't always start from one! You can count by twos, threes, fives, or tens.

How quickly can you count the shoes in this group? Count by twos, and you will be twice as quick, or count by threes, fives or tens to be faster still.

To play **Counting On**, the leader throws a handful of things onto the floor or table. The other players have a race to count them and say the right answer. The best way is to notice a group of things, and count on from that group. There might be six buttons together, so you can count on from six by ones, twos or fives.

5

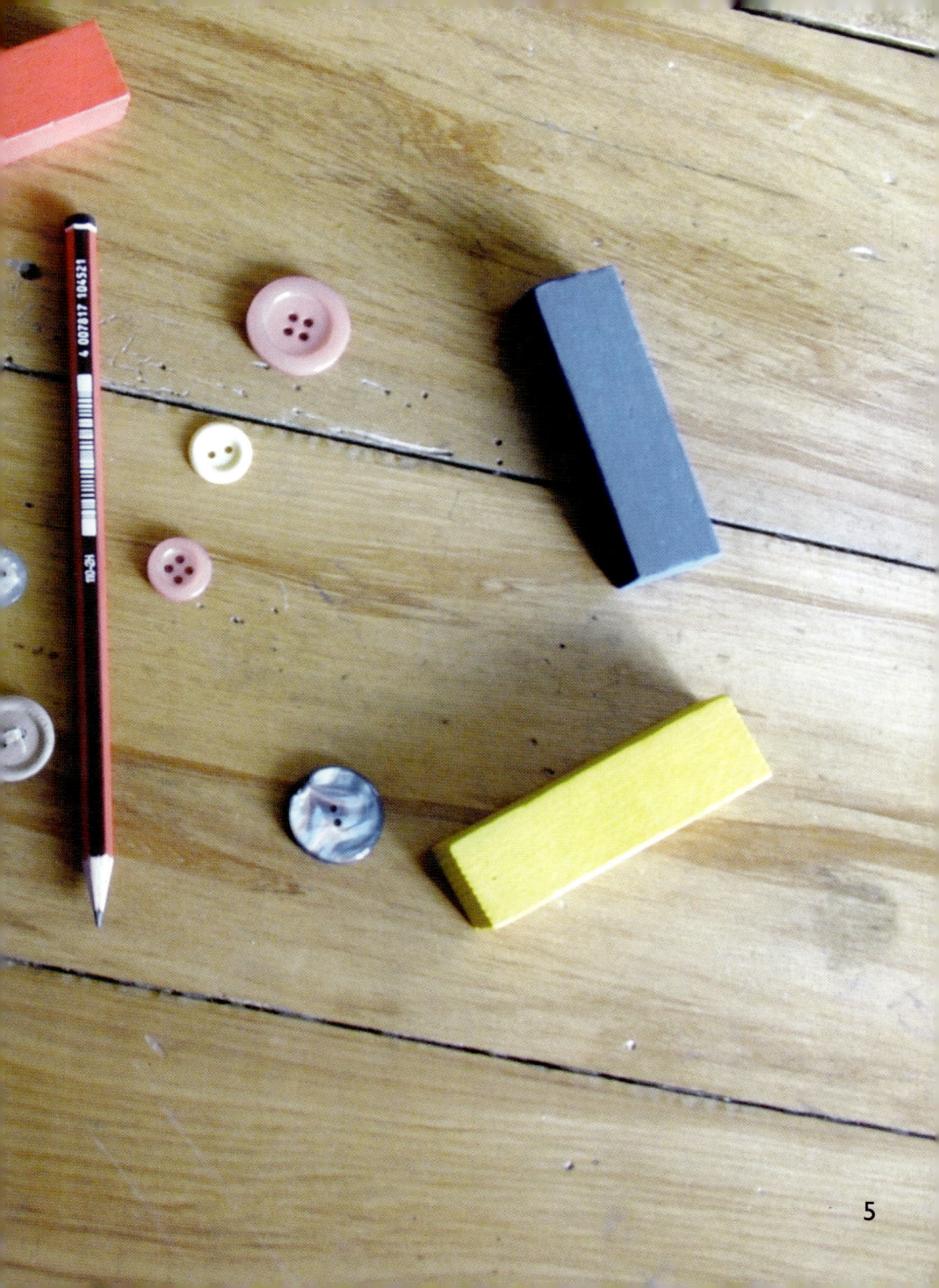

Guess the Number is fun! The leader hides a group of stones or buttons or other small things under his hand. The others try to guess how many. If the first guess is not right, the leader must give a clue, like "There are three less than that." The first player who works out the right answer becomes the next leader.

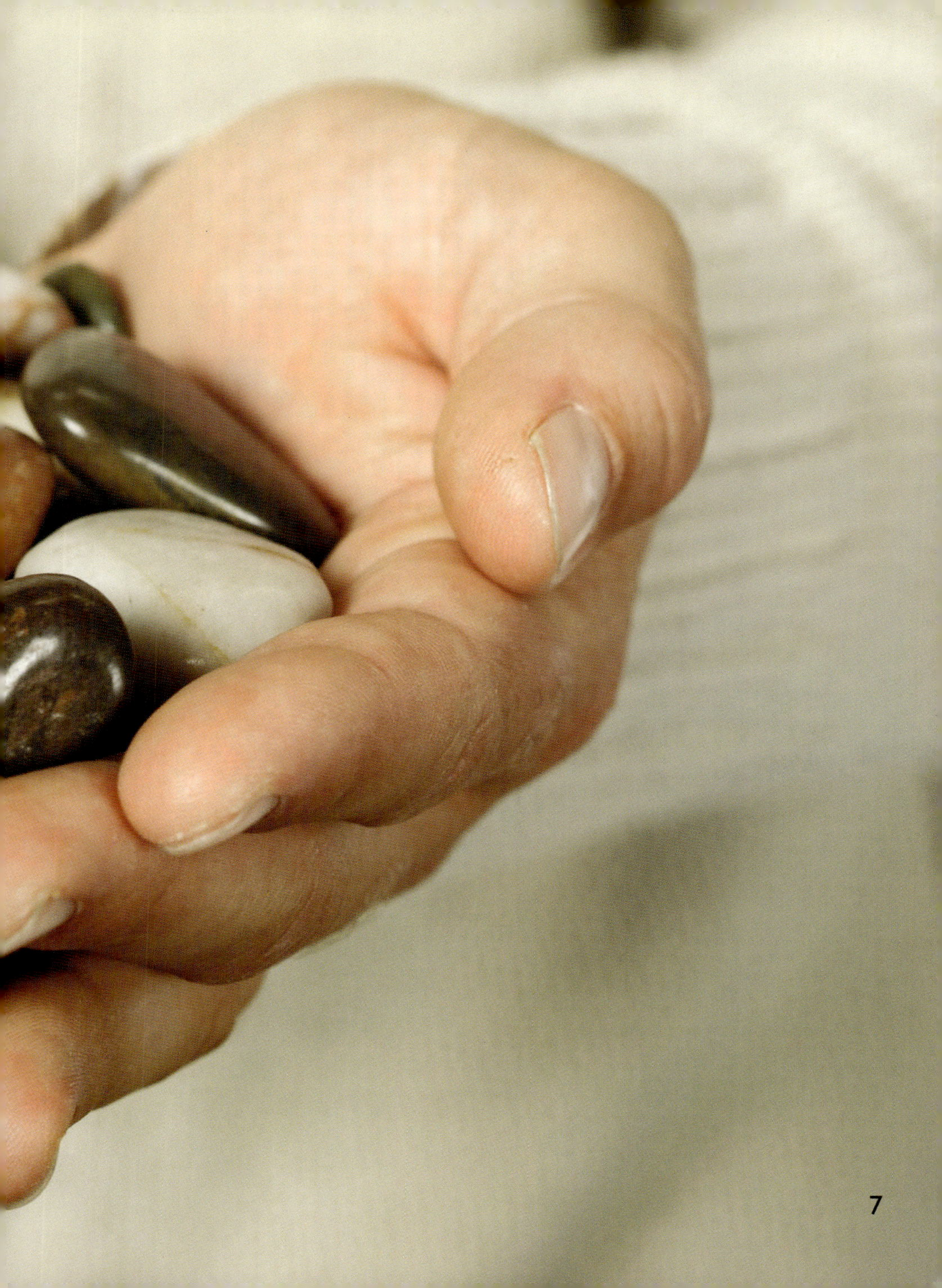

For **Memory Test**, a piece of paper is used to hide some groups of things, like stones and buttons and pencils. The players are told they have a short time to look at the things before they are covered over again. They must try to remember how many things were in each group.

9

You need to play fast in **Number Patterns**! The leader says or writes a list of numbers that have a pattern and asks, "What's next?" An easy pattern might be: 22, 33, 44, ? or 9, 7, 5, ?

The first person to notice the pattern gets a point and has the next turn. You will be able to think of much harder patterns, like 99, 89, 79, ?

For **Number Gap**, the leader writes a list of numbers and asks, "Where's the gap?"
He might write, " 18, 20, 24, 26", or " 12, 9, 6, 0". The players race to work out the missing number and win a point.

Who is the quickest at using doubles? Easy doubles sums like 2+2=4 and 6+6=12 can help when you play **Near Doubles**. You all know that 9+9=18, so you can answer fast if you are asked a sum that has only one different number: 9+8=17 and 9+10=19.

Would you like to play a fast game called **Hot Potato**? You only need a soft ball, which you use instead of a real hot potato! Make a circle with your friends and start by throwing the ball to one of them. Ask a sum like "Six plus eight?" as you throw the ball.

When he catches the "hot potato", your friend must answer quickly or he might get his fingers burned! He must throw the ball to another player, asking a new question. The winner will be the player with the most right answers, so he can start the next game.

To play **Age Sums,** you must write the ages of the people in your family or group. Who can make the most sums using those numbers? You will soon find out who is the best at playing number games!